I Need a Hug

Shoo!

Help!

Get away!
Spikes!

Get away!
Prickles!

Help!

No!
No!

No!
NO!
NO!

NO!

Shoo!
Spikes!

Get away!

Get away!
Help!
Shoo!
No!
Prickles!
Help!
NO!
Spikes!
No!
No!
NO!
Get away!
No!
NO!
Shoo!
No!
No!
Help!
Prickles!

For Patrycja

ISBN 978-1-338-53222-7

10 9 8 7 6 5 4 3 2 1   19 20 21 22 23

Printed in the U.S.A. 169
This edition first printing 2019

The artwork in this book is acrylic (with pens and pencils) on watercolor paper.
The type was set in Mrs Ant and Drina.

Aaron Blabey

I Need a Hug

Scholastic Inc.

I need a hug. Will you **cuddle** me, Ken?

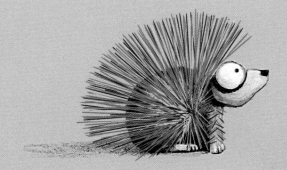

I need a hug.
Will you cuddle me, Joe?

Well, isn't this **lovely?**

Yes, how about this.

Hugs!
Aww!
Ahh! Aww!
Cuddles! Ooh!
KISS!
KISS! KISS!
Ooh!
Kisses!
Lovely!
Ooh!
Aww!
Hugs!
cuddles!
Aww!
Ahh!
Ooh, lovely

Ooh! Kiss!

Lovely

Kisses!

Cuddles!

Ahh!

Aww! Hugs!

Cuddles!

Ooh, Ahh!

lovely

Kisses!

KISS!

KISS!

KISS!

KISS!

Aww!

Hugs!

Lovely!

Cuddles!